W9-DGC-077
05724
STAND PRICE
$ 5.00

THE FIRST READER
& Three Plays

THE

Gertrude Stein

FIRST READER

& Three Plays

Decorated by Francis Rose

HOUGHTON MIFFLIN COMPANY BOSTON
THE RIVERSIDE PRESS CAMBRIDGE
1948

PRINTED BY HELY'S LIMITED DUBLIN IRELAND

THE FIRST READER

To Carl Van Vechten

Who did ask for a First Reader

LESSON ONE

A DOG SAID that he was going to learn to read. The other dogs said he could learn to bark but he could not learn to read. They did not know that dog, if he said he was going to learn to read, he would learn to read. He might be drowned dead in water but if he said that he was going to learn to read he was going to learn to read.

He never was drowned in water not dead drowned and he never did learn to read. Are there any children like that. One two three. Are there any children like that. Four five six. Are there any children like that. Seven eight nine are there any children like that.

Ten. Yes there are ten children like that and each one of the ten had a dog like that. Ten dogs like that and ten children like that, and the dogs and the children played tit for tat but there was no learning to read in that, not even if they each one of them was fat, fat just like that.

Next to this was a hare and next to the hare was a bird a daily bird. A daily bird is just a third of an ordinary bird, a daily bird being just a third was very likely heard and when he was heard well was it reading he heard, yes he heard them trying to learn to read the ten dogs and the ten children and as he the bird was a daily bird, and a daily bird is a third of a bird, he heard them every day trying to do less than a third of what they heard, so he said said the bird, I will get together ten daily birds and see who learns to read first ten children ten dogs or ten daily birds.

The first dog who tried to learn to read not the one who said he was going to learn to read that one did not need to have ten dogs to learn to read, he was the one dog who had it as a great need to learn to read. But would he learn to read. Who can tell, a bell learns to read, why not a dog, why not, the dog had tears in his eyes why not. A dog. But the first dog who really tried to learn to read he was a Saint Bernard a big dog so big that if he opened his mouth it was just the same as any word and when he said a word it was a big word. Saying a word even a big word is not the same as reading that word. Oh no said the daily bird no indeed it is not, not, not knot.

Just notice that if you say not knot, how do you know if you do not know how to read, which knot has a knot, and which not has not a knot. So you see you have to learn to read. The daily bird knew what was what.

The daily bird was all excited. He had heard a word. It might have been worm the word he heard but it was not. The word he heard was po-ta-toe. Sweet po-ta-toe, a lovely word, a sweet word, that was the word the daily bird heard. And he said hoe, no they mean hoe or ho and he said ha no they mean tea and he said toe oh yes toe, toe is that so. And then he said no it is not so it is potatoe and he smiled and smiled and said oh potatoe sweet potatoe that is so.

Daily birds like sweet potatoes that grow and if he could not read he could hear it said that they would hoe sweet potatoes in that bed.

Bed Bed, of course a bed when all is said is where you sleep, where any little boy or girl is put to sleep in a bed. But a bed when all is said is where they put potatoes to grow, and the daily bird knew that was so. Bed bed when any dog says bed bed, he means a cushion a basket a kennel or straw but when any child says bed he means a bed stead where he can lay himself down without a frown and with a pillow made of down he sleeps sweetly until he wakes up and comes down, down the stairs. Who cares which way down is spelt but it is spelt the same whether it is in the bed or out, remember all the little ten children were stout, but even so they did go in and out. But to the daily bird a bed when all is said is where the seeds are said to be in bed because they plant them so and so the daily bird when he heard po-ta-toe knew that that was a bed and so he said sweet potatoe bed, when all is said so sweet is a sweet potatoe bed and he heard the daily bird heard that word. Potatoe is what he heard and he read well he could not read but he read that they would plant potatoe seed in that bed and so he said oh how he said potatoe sweet oh sweet sweet sweet potatoe bed. And he was so pleased he was not dead, he was not in bed, and so he said, yes so he said, this the daily bird said.

Remember they plant sweet potatoes in the spring and eat them in the fall and that is all over when children are not fat but tall.

Oh dear yes that is all.

Think about spelling without yelling spell oh spell potatoe and know it is so. Potatoe, even if so has no e and potatoe has an e on toe. Potatoe.

So, now sew and so, so is so and sew is not so, you see to know whether sew is so or so is sew how necessary it is so that is to read is so necessary so it is. And read just think of read if red is read, and read is read, you see when all is said, just now read just then read, do you see even if a little boy or a little girl is very well fed if they do not read how can they know whether red is read and read is red. How can they know, oh no how can they know.

Dogs barking is different they bark louder that says so and so and they bark lower and that says and so and they make a little noise and that says so and so but well even if one dog said he would learn to read there was really no need and so well no, he would not learn to read, what did a dog care to know whether know is no, whether sew is so, whether read is red, what indeed did any little dog need to know, but a daily bird well a daily bird does not sing he twitters so, it is always just so, and so if he reads red or sees sew, even sow or even so so, even if it is printed on a shed and the daily bird sits upon the shed, no it is not for him to know the difference between so and sew and sow.

But a little boy and a little girl with or without a curl or a little boy with or without a toy, it would annoy a little boy oh surely it would annoy a little boy not to know that no is know that knot is not that sew is so and a little girl just even without a curl could not allow that if she saw a cow she would not bow because she did not know how to read a cow when she saw it said on a paper or on a shed that a cow is red. Think of the little girl with or without a curl who could not allow a cow to be a cow because she did not know how to read a cow. Think, oh think of that little girl now.

And so the daily bird was asleep on the bough and that is how it came to be now just now.

All alone a daily bird, it is a daily bird you can tell it is a daily bird because it is never heard. Daily daily daily bird.

Now the ten children who were stout were beginning to move about, and one said and another said and another said and another said and another said and another and another said and another said and another and another and they all ten said now if we count will we like it better that we see a bird a dog a cow or a hen, and when when they said a hen, they all began to cry and say no not I, I want to see a daily bird, a daily bird and that was all that was heard all the ten little children who were fat, they were just that, and being fat, they were afraid and being afraid they were not layed where they had seen a dog or cow oh dear not now, they would rather than read than weed, so that was what they knew, now remember about knew and new. Just remember, it makes one think of a cat just like that, it makes one think of a dog or a frog it makes one think of a man or a can it makes one think of also ran. Just think of that, a bird can twitter and sing and fly like anything, but a daily bird well a daily bird is a third of a bird, and eating is not everything, there is reading and writing, there is running and walking, there is sitting and hitting, there is barking and talking, there is white and black. Oh dear to read white and black. It looks very funny indeed it does. White And Black. It does look very funny indeed indeed it does.

Part Two

THE DAILY BIRD might be right.

Halve biscuits and have biscuits. Have to have biscuits. Have to halve biscuits. And have to have half a biscuit. Just think how to drink lemonade and have payed to have a biscuit or to have bread. When all is said. So you see said the daily bird, I like crumbs said the daily bird, crumbs of biscuits and crumbs of bread, but if the ten could not sleep in bed and when all is said could not read what is read, would I and the Daily Bird gave a sigh would I have crumbs of biscuits and bread and if I had not any crumbs then I would be dead, that is what the Daily Bird said. Dogs bark, it is dark and dogs bark and the Daily Bird well the Daily Bird had a friend, there were ten daily birds and three of them just three of them preferred the dark even if dogs the ten dogs did bark.

Bark, do you know what bark is, bark is what a dog does in the day time and in the dark and bark do you know what bark is, bark is what surrounds the wood on a tree and makes the wood all lovely for you and for me because all the ten little children quite stout could mount on a chair, perhaps the chair might break and feel like an earthquake because the ten little children were stout and if they were stout and the chair fell about then of course the stout ten little children would shout, and if and if not then what, they would carve

their names on the bark, not the bark of a dog not even the bark of their dog, the dog who said he would read not even on that dog's bark would they carve their names but on the bark of the tree, dear me.

LESSON TWO

A LITTLE BOY said I read a new word to-day.
What did you say.
The little boy said I read a new word to-day.
What word they said.
You guess he said.
Guess that's a new word.
No said the little boy no not that.
That they said, that is a word you never heard.
Oh no said the little boy don't I know that.
Well they said is it know.

No said the little boy no it is not know cant you guess he said.

Is it guess they said.

No he said no it is not guess not at all guess and not yes not at all yes, please guess.

Is it please they said no he said, not please, you are just anxious to please.

Is it anxious they said is anxious the new word you just read.

Yes said the little boy anxious it is, that is the new word I read. Yes they all said.

And they were so pleased that they had guessed.

Fortunately, fortunately is a long word, they would never have guessed fortunately, fortunately they were already to go and so it was yesterday.

Yesterday was a long word they would never have guessed yesterday, they might have guessed Wednesday or to-day but they would never have guessed yesterday.

One little boy said, I do not remember yesterday. Then the other little boy said I do I remember yesterday, yesterday is to-morrow. And they all laughed. They thought that was very funny.

By the time they had stopped laughing one little girl said, I was very wide awake yesterday.

Yesterday they all said.

And she began to cry. Yes she said I was very wide awake yesterday.

And then they all began to sing like anything.

I was very wide awake yesterday and they sang it and they sang and then the little girl said I said it, she was the one who had said it and they all said, yes she said it and then they all sang yes she said and they all laughed and laughed like anything.

By this time it was time to go home and they all said who said, and they all said I said and then some one said who was not a little boy or a little girl it is time to go home and they never said it is time to go home no little girl no little boy ever said it is time to go home. They can never have said it that way, you just try to say it that way any little boy any little girl, you have to learn to read before you can say it that way, it is time to go home.

There is something about that, no little boy no little girl who cannot read can say that.

LESSON THREE

WILLIE CAESAR was a wild boy. Whether he went or whether he would not go he always saw a w. Counting ws was a way for Willie Caesar to pass a whole day.

When he went away it made him wish that it was better weather. Which was why it was as well for him not to win whatever there was to be won. If he won well then he was one and in one there is no w.

But and butter is always but, but what. Now no one would ever think that Willie Caesar was attached to butter but he was. He ought to have been attached to cream because that would go with Caesar but no Willie was like that. Cream made him feel funny but butter, he did love butter, he loved butter better even than counting ws, and that is why he was so thin.

It seems funny that Willie Caesar was like that.

Willie Caesar loved to sit on a wall. He loved to wait for a wind, that is when he was flying kites and he was wonderfully well, and he was Willie Caesar and he would always wind up any piece of string and he was white with delight when the wind was whistling which is the way wind has. He liked the wind to be from the West which was his wish. Oh Willie said the West Wind, if your name was only Willie and not Caesar.

But Willy would not listen to the wind, his name was Willy Caesar and no matter even if the wind was from the west and was nice and windy he would not not have his name Caesar, he just would not.

Willy said that the wind from the West was welcome to go away if it only wanted Willy to be Willy and not Willy Caesar. Willy Caesar was what he was. He was a wild boy and he was called Willy Caesar because Willy Caesar was his name.

When he sat on a wall he was awake wide awake. Which was not a mistake.

When he sat on the wall and was wide awake he Willy Caesar said a wall will fall. Well will it.

If said Willie the wall will fall then unless I am as soft as butter I will be wounded by the stones and the clatter. And it will, it will fall, the wall will fall and Willy Caesar not being as soft as butter but only as thin as a pin was wounded by the stones and the clatter.

As he was falling off the wall he counted the last ws of all and that made how many? Wall, Well, Wall, Willy.

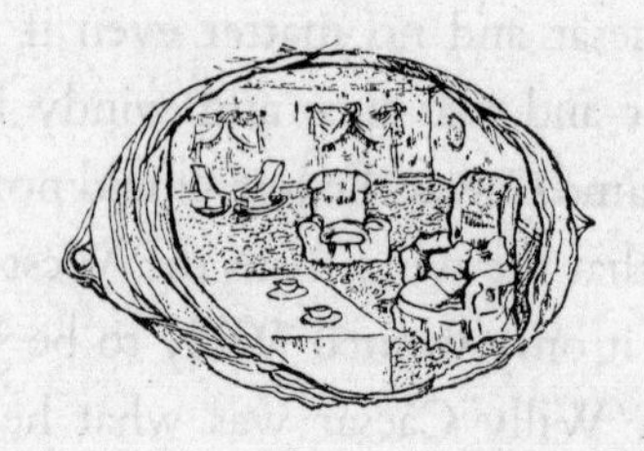

LESSON FOUR

BENJAMIN BABY.
Baby Benjamin.
Borrowing Baby Benjamin.

Benjamin was his name and he was not a baby. Little by little he was not a baby.

Saturday he was not a baby and Friday he was not a baby.

He was a baby Tuesday and Thursday.

He skipped Wednesday and Sunday. Wednesday and Sunday was when they borrowed Benjamin Baby.

So it was easy to notice which day it was. Was Benjamin a baby and you knew which two days it was. Was he not a baby then you knew which two days it was. Was he a borrowed baby then you knew which two it was.

And then there was Monday. Nobody ever knew there was a Monday, and yet they might know because on Monday there was no Benjamin Baby at all. There just was none.

How do you do said everybody on Monday and there was nobody to say how do you to because there was no Benjamin Baby at all.

More than that, Baby Benjamin had very little to say, he talked all the time but he had very little to say.

It does sometimes happen like that and when it does happen like that then Baby Benjamin has to wear a hat.

By all means when Baby Benjamin has to wear a hat and he always has to wear a hat, everybody wondered what day of the week it was. Was it a day of the week. You know sometimes a week has no days, when that happens joy abounds. But later well later they see Baby Benjamin and they know that a week has days nothing but days. So it was very easy to know Monday, no baby Benjamin, Tuesday Baby Benjamin was a baby Wednesday, Baby Benjamin was borrowed, Thursday Baby Benjamin was a baby Friday Baby Benjamin was not a baby Saturday Baby Benjamin was not a baby. Sunday they borrowed baby Benjamin. And so the week was over and everybody knew what day of the week every day had been, it was not necessary to read or write all they had to do was to watch Baby Benjamin, and nobody had anything else to do than to watch Baby Benjamin too and so everybody knew what day any day could be. Which was a pleasure too, and a trouble too but what use could they do. Baby Benjamin boo hoo.

LESSON FIVE

WILD FLOWERS.
Is Ivy on a tower a wild flower.
If white violets come out before blue
If they do.
Then it is true.

That the dew
Likes white better than blue.
If they knew.
White shows more than blue.
And then spring,
Spring makes water
Water makes spring,
And that makes everything
Just like anything.
If you see a yellow butterfly before a white one,
If you do
That means that the white one is coming too.
If you see two white butterflies before you see two
    yellow ones,
That means that everything is coming true.
Just for me and for you.
Believe it or not but you do.
That is what makes flowers come through
Yes they do.

LESSON SIX

JUST WHY Johnnie was Jimmie.
Just why Jimmie was Johnny.

Johnnie liked to measure everything, he liked to measure from here to there.

He liked to measure more than he liked to read yes indeed.

He measured his hair, he measured his share of a pear, he measured his feet he measured to where he would meet he measured his mother and his brother and he measured Jimmie.

And that was why Johnnie was Jimmie. Because Jimmie was measured by Johnnie, so that when Johnnie measured Jimmie they were back to back and when they were back to back because Johnnie was measuring Jimmie, Jimmie began to measure Johnnie and they were so back to back that neither Johnnie nor Jimmie could back. They were just back to back. Which was Johnnie and which was Jimmie or was Johnnie just Jimmie and was Jimmie just Johnny and just back to back.

Nobody knew if it was true that Jimmie was measuring Johnny or if Johnny was measuring Jimmie, nobody knew and this is true, that measuring everything from there to there makes it that nobody could tell whose hair was being measured there, was it Johnny or was it

Jimmie or was Jimmie just Johnny or was Johnny just Jimmie.

It is better to read than to measure even a treasure. If you read it is true just like me and like you but if you measure well how can you be so together that it is true that Johnny is just Jimmie and Jimmie is just Johnny and they both are through.

Better much better to read than to measure, measure from there to there, very much better.

LESSON SEVEN

BY THE TIME dates are ripe, by the time bananas are yellow, by the time olives are green by the time there is no in between, by the time it is time to get up and be sleepy by the time all the words are written by the time chocolate is sweet and sugar is eaten by the time

oranges grow and they all say so, by the time it is hot in summer and cold in winter by the time everything grows and everything shows by the time any boy sees by the time any girl knows by the time one is one and two is two by the time three and three make six, by the time shells have no fishes by the time water is blue by the time children are lost by the time too they are found through having been put to, work and play too, by the time it is not easy to have to do what they do by the time they are through by that time they two can read one and two and you and true, so they do.

LESSON EIGHT

THE THIRTEENTH of March was a day when it was dangerous to play.

The moon was full that is to say the moon was full of moon.

The water tide came in and out and everywhere all about it was dangerous to go in and out.

A little boy said he would all the same, the little boy had a name. But nobody said his name. It was just better not to say the same.

And so when everybody stayed at home because the thirteenth of March is a day like that, this little boy accompanied only by a cat and without a hat went out, the round of the moon was just turning about and he began to shout. And just than a fat hen saw a trout. It was a little trout who was just getting to go about, and the fat hen said when I see that trout I will be a duck and go about in the water and eat that trout. This was a mistake the fat hen would not have thought of doing so if it had not been that it was March the thirteenth a day when it is dangerous to be out, so the hen thinking she was a duck in a theatre and that the water was not real went after the baby trout and the fat hen was drowned dead before she could get out when she had found out that she was not a duck in a theatre but a hen in the water.

So the little boy who had a name saw that so he put on his hat and tried to go home again. But and that is why it is dangerous to be out on the thirteenth of March, the rain came again and before the little boy who had a name could say when he was drowned like the hen. This is what happens on the thirteenth of March, no little boy should say when then.

LESSON NINE

THE SUN IS very full of sunshine which is very pleasant just at nine, when the wash is hanging out on the line. Turkeys are wild and turkeys are tame which is a shame. Peacocks too and they are blue and if all this is true who are you.

This is what the sun said when after having been up since nine he thought of setting time after time, but they said no, what is there to show that the sun has sunshine if he is setting all the time. So the sun said he would shine even if it was nine and he did just as if he was a lid which he was because there was a cover which did cover all around the sun cover the sun all up and after that there was no bother nobody had to get up even at nine. Anyway there was no sunshine, not yesterday. It is different to-day. Thank you very much for such.

LESSON TEN

THIS IS THE WAY they talked. Who said which first. If he said which first, which which did he say first. He scratched his head and he said, for me just for me I like which first. Well that was very funny not just

for money but that was very funny, very very funny. Then they began to think well not really to think, you know what thinking is, you look up and you look down and you think and when you think well when you think you know which says which first. Each one who thinks thinks he said which first. Not to be neglected they think again. And when they think again, well now it is extraordinary, but when they think again which is extraordinary then better and better and more and more they know which one said which first. Now which one did. That is the question. Which one said which first.

Almost at once each one said which first. Almost at once. And then it was very kind, it was very kind of each one very kind of each one to think that they said which first. Very kind indeed, yes indeed, very kind. It was very kind very kind indeed, of each one of them very kind indeed of each one of them to think that each one of them said which first. Very kind, indeed very kind, indeed very kind indeed.

Yes very very kind.

LESSON ELEVEN

NOW WHEN butter is careless, and milk is anxious, and potatoes are mournful and spinach is angry and carrots are sudden and cabbage is morose and eggs are polite well then when that happy time has come it is very necessary that every little boy and every little girl says how do you do, and when every little girl and every little boy has said how do you do, how does every little boy and how does every little girl do. They just say very well I thank you that is if they know how to say that but if they do not know how to say that they just say well they just do not say, they do not say how they are. Imagine that when every little boy and every little girl when every little girl and every little boy says how do you do, well then nobody sometimes just nobody does know how they do do. Do first think about that.

It is almost quite almost necessary, almost quite necessary to think about that.

By this time they are all there, believe it or not as you like but it is true, by this time they are all there, all there by this time.

It is very likely that they prefer peas to spinach, it is very likely and it is very likely that they prefer water to daisies very likely, it is even more likely that if they walk and there is mud, that there is mud where they walk. What is more likely. Well really nothing is more likely. Nothing is as much likely as that. Nothing. Just think of that.

LESSON TWELVE

SOME sheep are loving and some sheep are not.
What what.
Can canaries cry.
Not if four pansy buds can try

To be better and better.
Better than butter
Butter what

Butter cups
Butter cups are yellow
So can pansies be
Which make pansies come to see
That butterflies come sooner than a bee.
Butterflies butter cups
Butter butter nuts
Butter Butter
If sheep are loving
What does it matter,
Cows make butter
Sheep can try
But it makes them cry,
Butter butter,
So they stamp their feet,
Which are neat,
But not better than butter.
Oh butter oh butter,
A sheep can butt her
Yes she can yes she does
Loving as she is,
A sheep can butt her
Which she does
When a little dog is yellow
Yes she does
She does butt her.
Butter.
For which we say any day butter is better.

LESSON THIRTEEN

JENNY IS a little girl with blue eyes. She was fond of flowers but she was discouraged about picking them. Whenever she picked them pretty blue flowers or rosy flowers or pink flowers or white flowers and she held them in her hand or she tied them up in a handkerchief, by the time she got home they were all gone, there were none left and she never knew what had become of them. She thought it was very funny but it was so all the same. She thought it had to do with her hands and so she was always comparing her hands with the hands of little girls who brought home flowers but her hands and the hands of the other little girls looked just the same. She did not know what it was but there it was, it was just like that, no matter how often she picked flowers and however carefully she held them in her hand or her hands when she came home her hands were empty, there were no flowers in them.

Now why was it.

If anybody could tell her would it help her or would it not.

LESSON FOURTEEN

ONCE UPON A TIME there was a farm on a hill, and there was a tower there, and there was a large farmer's wife there and as she stood there she saw a soldier passing. He looked at her and she said to him young soldier what are you doing. I am just passing said the soldier. And she said to him and why are you all alone. I am all alone said the young soldier because I am lonesome. Why are you lonesome said the farmer's wife. Because said the soldier I come from a place where they have been bombarding. And are your people dead, she asked. Oh no, said the soldier, they are alive but they have no homes, all their homes have been bombarded to nothing and the church where I went to see a friend married just before I left home, that too is all bombarded to nothing. Just then the farmer came along and he said to the soldier come in. And they sat him down at the table and they talked together until evening and the young soldier went back to his garrison. He was still alone but was he less lonesome. No he was still lonesome.

LESSON FIFTEEN

BELIEVE IT OR NOT it is true.
They need what they need which is blue.

And the wind blew and they blew and they whistled for you and then well almost always it was true that just as much as ever they could they would just as much as ever they could and by the time it was often well just by the time it was often they began to soften and much as they liked it they went away twice. Now going away once is not often but going away twice just going away twice makes them not like mice. They think very carefully whether mice or in the house or out of doors they do think very carefully twice about mice.

You know it does get to be a habit to do everything twice. If you do it in private you will do it in public, but it works the other way so they say, if you do it in public you will do it in private so you have to be awfully careful just most awfully careful about that word twice. You do whether you do or whether you do not like mice. You do have to be careful about twice. Twice is one of the things one of the things about which you have to be careful.

Twice. You have to be careful twice, once and then twice. How nice.

LESSON SIXTEEN

A Play

Act One

A LITTLE BOY was standing in front of a house and opposite him was a blackberry vine. The blackberry vine had a very pleasant expression.

How do you do little boy, it said.

Very well I thank you said the little boy only I am all alone.

Not like me said the blackberry vine I am never alone.

No said the little boy not even in winter.

No said the blackberry vine, not even in winter, I am never alone come and see said the blackberry vine always with the pleasant expression.

Just then a little girl came along and she saw the little boy and she said to him how do you do little boy.

The little boy said very well I thank you only I am all alone.

Not when I am here said the little girl if I am here then you are not alone.

Yes said the blackberry vine and it had a pleasant

expression yes he is a stupid little boy he does not understand anything.

Act Two

The little girl took the little boy's hand, she said now let us go away and play.

Not at all said the little boy I cannot go away and play because I am all alone.

Beside said the blackberry vine still with its pleasant expression if you went away I could not go along, a blackberry vine is never alone and so it cannot roam.

Well said the little girl I see no reason why the little boy and I should stay with the blackberry vine.

But said the little boy I do not stay with the blackberry vine, because if I stayed with the blackberry vine I would not be alone and I am said the little boy I am all alone.

He is said the blackberry vine he is a stupid little boy he just does not understand anything.

The little girl was not pleased with the blackberry vine, she did not like his pleasant expression not at all, but since the little boy would not come at her call she had to stay with the little boy and the blackberry vine.

Act Three

The little boy sighed, he said it is bad to be all alone.

But said the little girl and the blackberry vine, not at all little boy not at all, you are not all alone not at all alone, you stupid little boy, stupid stupid little boy.

I wonder said the little girl I wonder is he all alone I wonder.

And the blackberry vine began to cry, it still had the same pleasant expression but it began to cry. Oh my, it said perhaps I am all alone perhaps if I try I might only sigh and not have anybody else be by. Perhaps the little boy knows why.

And the little girl said not at all not at all not at all. The little boy is not alone, about the blackberry vine well it can do as it likes but the little boy no I will show the little boy until he knows it is so, and if the blackberry vine scratches, and I put on ashes on the scratches the little boy will know I am I and so he will not cry because he is all alone.

And so that is what the little girl did, she gave the little boy a shove, and the blackberry vine still with its pleasant expression made the little boy whine, oh my he said it scratches, of course it scratches said the little girl, it has torn my dress oh yes.

Oh yes said the little boy well then I guess I am not alone so let us go and play.

That is what I say said the little girl.

And the blackberry still with the same pleasant expression said go away or stay it is all the same to me, I am never alone and it is true, no matter what you can say winter or summer night or day a blackberry vine is never alone and it always has the same pleasant expression.

The little boy and the little girl had gone away to play.

LESSON SEVENTEEN

CUPS AND SAUCERS. Tables and chairs.

It was no credit to Johnny and Emma no credit to them not to break the cups and saucers not to cut the tables nor themselves with the knives. No credit to them.

They were very careful to sit down on chairs, they might have sat on the stairs but they did not, they were very careful to sit on chairs.

Noises were heard.

When they heard the noises they thought the noises were on the stairs so they got off their chairs and they took the knives and they went behind the tables and they waited.

If they waited long enough they would hear the noises again but they did not wait long enough they began to make noises of their own. Johnny made his and Emma made hers and together they made each others. They thought they were waiting but they were really making noises.

And so even if the noises came again they would not know their knives clattered so, their chairs moved so their tables wiggled so.

And so just when it was all so, the noises came and they did not hear them come.

The noises were on the stairs one by one, and one by one the stairs were run, they were run by the noises that came one by one.

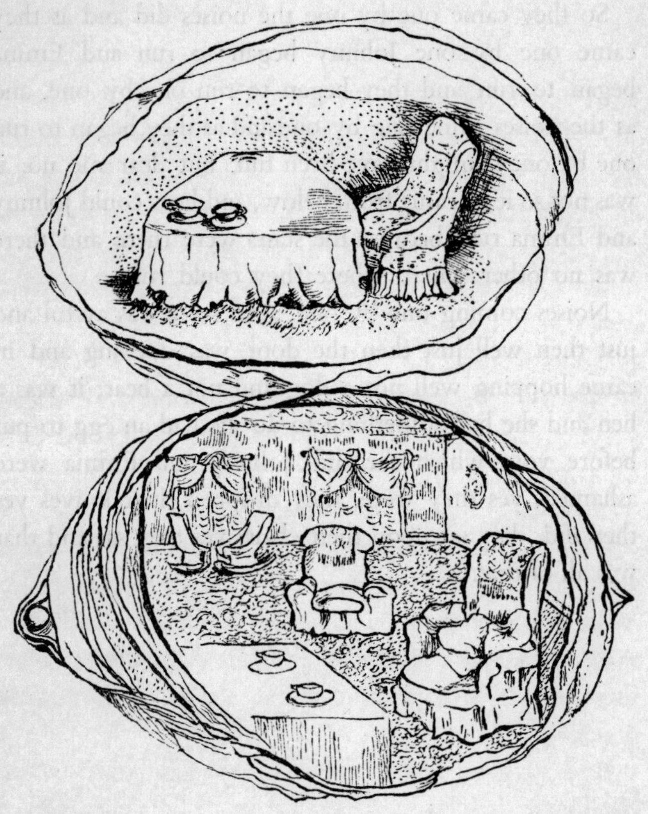

Nothing is so bad as noises that come one by one.

Johnny and Emma were two and so they thought that two would stop noises coming one by one. But no, the noises said no, the noises said just so, we will come from below said the noises and we will come one by one, one by one.

So they came one by one the noises did and as they came one by one Johnny began to run and Emma began to run and they began to run one by one, and as the noises came one by one and as they began to run one by one it might have been fun, but dear me no, it was not so it all came from below, and how could Johnny and Emma run, because the stairs were there and there was no other where where they could run.

Noises coming one by one. And so it was awful and just then well just then the door was opening and in came hopping well not a dog and not a bear, it was a hen and she had something to do she had an egg to put before you, which she did. Johnny and Emma were ashamed, yes they were, they dropped their knives yes they did, they sat upon their chairs yes they sat and that was all of that.

LESSON EIGHTEEN

A Ballad

A BIG BIRD flying high
In the sky
Makes little birds sitting by
Know that they must do or die.
It was in the woods and it was dark,
And dogs bark,
But little birds know that dogs are there
There where they cannot stare
Into the nests where birdies are,
But a big bird that flies on high
Even when leaves are everywhere
He can see right down from the sky
And see even nests hidden with care
And so they do not dare
The little birds do not dare
To let the big bird fly too low
Because he will take their little ones so
Right in his claws and away will go
To give them to eat to his own big birds which need

to eat and have a treat of littler birds which are so sweet.
And so.
As I said.
And as you have read
When a big bird flies high
The little birds know they must do or die.
And so they do
And to be true

It is not the little birds that die but the big bird that flies high in the sky.
The big bird is there,

The little birds with all care all together fly over there.
They fly higher and higher.
And higher and higher,
And they come nearer and nearer
One after the other
Until the big bird begins to feel queer
And wonder what is all the bother.
And so the little birds in a big number,
Come on hitting the big bird on the head
And hoping he is dead.
And another comes down and another comes down.
And the big bird begins to frown,
And he tries to get away
But no there is no way,
The little birds say,
If he gets away he will come back another day,
And so one after the other so
Quickly that they seem like bees,
Come down and hit the big bird on the crown,
And slowly the big bird sinks lower down,
And down and down,
And the little birds begin to frown
And they begin to know
The big bird will go down,
And down and down,
And at last no more,
The big bird can soar,
And he falls down and down

And the little birds keeping hitting at him down down and the big bird at last has fallen down and the lake is there and he will drown.

And all the little birds fly away to tell their little birds to stay all the danger has gone away.

And this does happen any day just like I say.

LESSON NINETEEN

WHICH IS, said a wild pen.
Which is,
A wild pen is different from a pencil,
and it is even different from a slate pencil.

A wild pen is a pen that makes blots that makes dots that makes spots.

That is what a wild pen is.

And a wild pen is a pen that can get wilder and wilder and when it gets wilder and wilder it does get wilder and wilder and instead of saying how do you do it says you had better not have said how do you do because if you have said how do you do how do you know what a wild pen will do.

A wild pen will do anything it just will do anything, it will go round and around, it will run away, it will give ink away, it will change its name, it will fasten a stain on a finger so strong that the stain will not go away for ever so long. A wild pen is wilder than anything, it is wilder than a cat or a cow or a bat or a tiger or an eagle or a rat, it is wilder than anything and anybody knows how wild is that.

That is what a pen is when it is wild and so a pen should be told that a pen is a thing to be sold, that a pen should never be bold that a pen should never be cold.

A pen is naturally a pen, and so anyone who has a pen should be firm with that pen and never let that pen be bold never let that pen be wild because that is awful for a child to have a pen that is wild awful for a child, just awful for a child.

LESSON TWENTY

BE VERY CAREFUL of how do you do.
Be very careful of when this you see remember me.
Be very careful of very well I thank you
Be very careful of please can I go out.
Be very careful of what do you want.
Be very careful of how many eggs are there in it.
Be very careful of what have you in your pocket.
Be very careful of how can you hear me,
Be very careful of one two three
Be very careful of how old are you,
Very careful.
Be very careful of Many many can tickle you
Be very careful again be very careful of how do you do.
Very careful of How do you do.
By this time they were all tired of being careful.
And so
They were told so
They were told to be very careful they were told so.
Be very careful of can you guess.
Be very careful of never the less
Be very careful of it is hot it is cold
Be very careful of I want to be told
Be very careful of next time

Be very careful of at once

But be most careful of all of how to fall when running away.

Be very careful I say all night and all day,

Be very careful of at work or in play,

Be very careful, yes I say be very careful very very careful, just as careful, as careful can be, when this you see be as careful as you can be.

And all the little girls and all the little boys said yes we will be you will see we will be as careful as careful can be.

THE THREE PLAYS

IN A GARDEN

A Tragedy In One Act

LUCY WILLOW

PHILIP HALL

KIT RACOON

Scene: A garden with a bench.

LUCY WILLOW: I am thinking how to be a queen, I am not thinking about how to be a princess, I am thinking about how to be a queen. I am thinking not about being Lucy Willow but how to be a queen.

Philip Hall on one side and Kit Racoon on the other each carrying a battle-axe come behind and listen.

LUCY WILLOW: It would be lovely to be a queen, I must be a queen, I will be a queen.

Philip Hall and Kit Racoon rush forward each one on a side and they fall on their knees and they stretch out their hands and they both say:

Be a queen, be a queen be my queen.

LUCY WILLOW: What do you mean. I am a queen but not your queen, you (*pointing at Philip Hall*) you are Philip Hall and that is all, how can you be a king, but I (*she gives a sigh*) I am a queen oh it is so lovely to be a queen.

PHILIP HALL: (*jumping to his feet*) I am a king and how can I tell I can tell because when I hit my chest I ring like a bell, that is what happens when you are a king, (*and then falling on his knees*) oh queen be a queen be my queen.

KIT RACOON (*jumping to his feet he had been murmuring*): Be a queen be my queen. I am a king and I do not have to change my name I can be a king all the same I am Kit Racoon the first, all you have to do is to be the first and then you are a king, listen to me I am king Kit Racoon the first (*and falling on his knees*) and you are my queen, be a queen be my queen.

Lucy Willow: You both say you are a king but that does not prove anything, now I know I am a queen, and it is lovely to be a queen, and I must be a queen I will be a queen, I am a queen, but you two you just say you are a king, that does not prove anything.

Philip Hall jumps to his feet Kit Racoon continues kneeling murmuring: be a queen be my queen.

Philip Hall: Aha you say you are a queen, aha, but where is your crown, look at me (*and out of his pocket he takes a gold crown*) aha, I am a king I have a crown (*putting it on his head*) I am a king but you you a queen where is your crown, Aha.

Lucy Willow (*shrinking back terrified*): Oh perhaps I am no queen perhaps I am only Lucy Willow lovely Lucy Willow but no queen (*and then drawing herself up proudly*) crown or no crown I know I am a queen.

Kit Racoon (*jumps to his feet*): Aha you a queen, look at me Kit Racoon the first and a crown (*he takes a gold crown out of his pocket and puts it on his head*) Kit Racoon the first and every inch a king with his crown (*and then falling on his knees*) but all the same be a queen dear be my queen.

Philip Hall (*on his knees too with a crown on his head*): Lovely queen be a queen be my queen.

Lucy Willow (*perplexed*): I am a queen I know I am a queen I have no crown but I know I am a queen but how can I be your queen, I am only one queen and you are two kings because you each have a crown, what can I do I can only frown (*and she frowns*).

Both the kings jump up and seize their battle-axes.

PHILIP HALL: I will kill him and then there will only be one king, and I will be that king and you will be a queen my queen. I will fight like anything and (*handing her his gold crown*) here is my gold crown hold it so that it will not get torn.

Lucy Willow takes the crown and holds it lovingly.

KIT RACOON (*flourishing his axe*): Wait and see Kit Racoon the first can kill like lightning, all he has to do is to hit another king with his axe and that other king will be dead like anything. Here queen here is my crown, do not let it fall down.

The two kings begin to fight and they fight hard with their axes and they are both killed and as they are dying they stretch out their hands to her and cry:

As I die be my queen be a queen be my queen (*and they both die*).

LUCY WILLOW (*slowly looking at the two crowns in her hand*): It is lovely to be a queen, I must be a queen, I am a queen, I can tell by feeling, I am a queen and it is lovely to be a queen (*and she slowly crowns herself with the double crown while the curtain falls*).

THREE SISTERS WHO ARE NOT SISTERS

A Melodrama

JENNY, HELEN *and* ELLEN

SAMUEL *and* SYLVESTER

WE ARE THREE sisters who are not sisters, not sisters. We are three sisters who are orphans.

We are three sisters who are not sisters because we have not had the same mother or the same father, but because we are all three orphans we are three sisters who are not sisters.

Enter two brothers.

We are two brothers who are brothers, we have the same father and the same mother and as they are alive and kicking we are not orphans not at all, we are not even tall, we are not brave we are not strong but we never do wrong, that is the kind of brothers we are.

JENNY: And now that everybody knows just what we are what each one of us is, what are we going to do.

SYLVESTER: What are we going to do about it.

JENNY (*impatiently*): No not what are we going to do about it there is nothing to do about it, we are three sisters who are not sisters, and we are three orphans and you two are not, there is nothing to do about that. No what I want to know is what are we going to do now. Now what are we going to do.

SAMUEL: I have an idea a beautiful idea, a fine idea, let us play a play and let it be a murder.

JENNY:
HELEN: Oh yes let's.
ELLEN:

SYLVESTER: I won't be murdered or be a murderer, I am not that kind of a brother.

SAMUEL: Well nobody says you are, all you have to do is to be a witness to my murdering somebody.

HELEN: And who are you going to murder.

SAMUEL: You for choice. Let's begin.

ELLEN: Oh I am so glad I am not a twin, I would not like to be murdered just because I had a sister who was a twin.

JENNY: Oh don't be silly, twins do not have to get murdered together, let's begin.

Scene 2

A room slightly darkened, a couch, and a chair and a glass of water, the three sisters sitting on the couch together, the light suddenly goes out.

JENNY: Look at the chair.

HELEN: Which chair.

JENNY: The only chair.

ELLEN: I can't see the only chair.

JENNY (*with a shriek*): Look at the only chair.

All three together: There is no chair there.

SAMUEL: No there is no chair there because I am sitting on it.

SYLVESTER: And there is no him there because I am sitting on him.

JENNY: Which one is going to murder which one.
SAMUEL: Wait and see.

Suddenly the light goes up there is nobody in the room and Sylvester is on the floor dead.

[CURTAIN]

ACT II

Scene I

The light is on.

Sylvester is on the floor dead.
Jenny is asleep on the couch.
She wakes up and she sees Sylvester on the floor dead.

Oh he is dead Sylvester is dead somebody has murdered him, I wish I had a sister a real sister oh it is awful to be an orphan and to see him dead, Samuel killed him, perhaps Helen killed him, perhaps Ellen but it should be Helen who is dead and where is Helen.

She looks under the bed and she bursts out crying.

There there is Helen and she is dead, Sylvester killed her and she killed him. Oh the police the police.

There is a knock at the door and Samuel comes in dressed like a policeman and Jenny does not know him.

JENNY: Yes Mr. Policeman I did kill them I did kill both of them.

SAMUEL: Aha I am a policeman but I killed both of them and now I am going to do some more killing.

JENNY (*screaming*): Ah ah.

And the lights go out and then the lights go up again and Jenny is all alone, there are no corpses there and no policeman.

JENNY: I killed them but where are they, he killed them but where is he. There is a knock at the door I had better hide.

She hides under the bed.

Scene 2

SAMUEL (*as a policeman comes in*): Aha there is nobody dead and I have to kill somebody kill somebody dead. Where is somebody so that I can kill them dead.

He begins to hunt around and he hears a sound, and he is just about to look under the bed when Ellen comes in.

ELLEN: I am looking for Helen who is not my twin so I do not have to be murdered to please her but I am looking for her.

Samuel the policeman comes out of the corner where he has been hiding.

SAMUEL: Aha you killed her or aha you killed him, it does not make any difference because now I am going to do some killing.

ELLEN: Not me dear kind policeman not me.

SAMUEL: I am not a policeman I am a murderer, look out here I come.

The light goes out. When it comes on again, the policeman is gone and Ellen murdered is on the floor.

Jenny looks out timidly from under the bed and gives a shriek:

Oh another one and now I am only one and now I will be the murdered one.

And timidly she creeps back under the bed.

[CURTAIN]

ACT III

Jenny under the bed. Samuel this time not like a policeman but like an apache comes creeping in.

SAMUEL: Aha I am killing some one.

JENNY (*under the bed*): He can't see me no he can't, and anyway I will kill him first, yes I will.

Suddenly the room darkens and voices are heard.

I am Sylvester and I am dead, she killed me, every one thinks it was Samuel who killed me but it was not it was she.

HELEN'S VOICE: I am Helen and I am dead and everybody thinks it was Samuel who killed me but not at all not all not at all it was she.

A THIRD VOICE: I am Ellen and I am dead, oh so dead, so very very dead, and everybody thinks it was Samuel but it was not it was not Samuel it was she oh yes it was she.

The light goes up and Jenny alone looks out fearfully into the room from under the bed.

JENNY: Oh it was not Samuel who killed them it was not, it was she and who can she be, can she be me. Oh horrible horrible me if I killed all three. It cannot be but perhaps it is, (*and she stretches up very tall*) well if it is then I will finish up with him I will kill him Samuel and then they will all be dead yes all dead but I will not be dead not yet.

The light lowers and Samuel creeps in like an apache.

SAMUEL: They say I did not kill them they say it was she but I know it was me and the only way I can prove that I murdered them all is by killing her, aha I will find her I will kill her and when I am the only one the only one left alive they will know it was I that killed them all, I Samuel the apache.

He begins to look around and suddenly he sees a leg of Jenny sticking out under the bed. He pulls at it.

SAMUEL: Aha it is she and I will kill her and then they will know that I Samuel am the only murderer.

He pulls at her leg and she gives a fearful kick which hits him on the temple. He falls back and as he dies,

SAMUEL: Oh it is so, she is the one that kills every one, and that must be so because she has killed me, and that is what they meant, I killed them each one, but as she was to kill me, she has killed all of them all of them. And she has all the glory, Oh Ciel.

And he dies.

Jenny creeps out from under the bed.

JENNY: I killed him yes I did and he killed them yes he did and now they are all dead, no brothers no sisters no orphans no nothing, nothing but me, well there is no use living alone, with nobody to kill so I will kill myself.

And she sees the glass of water.

JENNY: Aha that is poison.

She drinks it and with a convulsion she falls down dead. The lights darken and the voices of all of them are heard.

We are dead she killed us, he killed us sisters and brothers orphans and all he killed us she killed us she killed us he killed us and we are dead, dead dead.

The lights go up and there they all are as in the first scene.

JENNY: Did we act it are we dead, are we sisters, are we orphans, do we feel funny, are we dead.

SYLVESTER: Of course we are not dead, of course we never were dead.

SAMUEL: Of course we are dead, can't you see we are dead, of course we are dead.

HELEN (*indignantly*): I am not dead, I am an orphan and a sister who is not a sister but I am not dead.

ELLEN: Well if she is not dead then I am not dead. It is very nice very nice indeed not to be dead.

JENNY: Oh shut up everybody, shut up, let's all go to bed, it is time to go to bed orphans and all and brothers too.

And they do.

[FINIS]

LOOK AND LONG

A Play In Three Acts

FOUR COUSINS

TWO BROTHERS: OLIVER, SILLY

TWO COUSINS: MURIEL, SUSIE

AN APPARITION

Scene: In front of a house with trees.

Enter Oliver, profoundly sad, he stops and looks about and folds his arms and looks up at the sky.

OLIVER: I wonder, oh I wonder.

Silence.

From the other side enters Muriel, she too is profoundly sad and her eyes are cast down on the ground as she stands. Suddenly she sees a spider.

MURIEL: Araignee de matin, fait chagrin, and it is morning.

She stops and crouches behind a chair in an agony of despair.

In rush Susie and Silly.

SUSIE: Oh I have I have seen a goat a white goat and I milked him oh a lovely goat a lovely white goat.

SILLY: Silly Susie a goat is a she if she gives milk to three, beside it was not a goat, it was a chicken and it was an egg not milk even if it was white do you see.

Silly and Susie dance around and suddenly they see Oliver that is to say they bump against him.

SUSIE: Oh I thought he was a tree. When this you see remember me.

Oliver pays no attention he continues to gloom looking up at the sky with folded arms.

SILLY: Oh look Susie look what is there, there behind that chair.

Susie and Silly steal around quietly behind the chair and there is Muriel her eyes fixed on the ground in despair.

MURIEL (*murmurs*): The spider the spider oh the spider it is not there.

OLIVER (*gives a start*): It was a cuckoo and (*with a bitter cry*) I have no money in my purse no money anywhere. Oh why did that cuckoo try to cry when I had no money no money, none.

MURIEL: No money.

SUSIE AND SILLY: No money.

OLIVER: No money, none.

Just then there was a funny noise and in the middle of the four of them was a dancing apparition.

All together: Oh (*and they watch her dance*).

SUSIE: Is it pretty.

OLIVER: Is it ugly.

MURIEL: Who is it.

SILLY: Where does it come from.

APPARITION (*dancing*): I come from the moon, I come from the sun and I come to look at you one by one.

And then suddenly stopping she points a finger at Oliver:

You you, one of these days you will split in two, you, you.

OLIVER (disdainfully): I wonder.

APPARITION: You will wonder when it comes like thunder that you will split in two all through.

And suddenly pointing her finger at Muriel:

APPARITION: And you.

MURIEL: Well what of it I have no share nor any care of any thing that happens to him.

APPARITION: No but you will get thin, get thin oh so thin, that you can slip through a ring and when you slip through a ring nobody can find you nobody can find where you have been nobody, nobody, nobody not even he and this is what the spider said and he was red the spider and this is what he said.

MURIEL: Oh (*and she began to sigh*) Oh my.

APPARITION (*pointing one finger at Susie and another at Silly*): Silly will turn into Willy and Susie will turn into an egg and Willie will sit on the egg, and so they will wed Willie and the egg, although the egg was bad. Oh dear (*the apparition began to giggle and giggle*) oh dear (*and she faded away giggling*).

OLIVER (*gloomily*): I don't care for my share.

MURIEL (*with a gentle sigh*): I like to be thin, it is so interesting.

Susie and Silly holding hands just laugh and laugh and the curtain falls.

ACT II

Oliver comes in very gloomily and all tied up with string.

OLIVER: I'll fool her, when I split in two if I do this string will hold me together whatever I do, so nobody can know not even she, and she is ugly, that I am not one but two, she'll see.

Muriel coming in and in each hand a huge bottle of milk.

MURIEL: No I won't, yes I will, it would be a thrill to be thin and go through a ring, but I'll fool her yes I will, hullo Oliver are you in two, then I will be as thin as either one of you.

OLIVER (*gloomily*): Go to bed.

MURIEL: Go to bed yourself, what do I care what happens to you.

OLIVER: You do too.

Muriel begins to cry: Boohoo.

Just then Susie and Silly come in giggling.

SUSIE: I am an egg and I am cracked and Silly is Willy and he is so silly, see me crack, hear me crack.

SILLY: And the egg you are is addled at that.

And they giggle and giggle and the other two continue to be gloomy.

SILLY: Hush I hear a noise, let us each get behind a tree so she cannot see and then we will know what she can do. Hush. (*And they each get behind a tree*).

The apparition comes in disguised as an old woman picking up sticks. As she picks them up she dances.

APPARITION: One stick is one two sticks are two three sticks are three four sticks are four, four sticks are four, three sticks are three, two sticks are two, one stick is one. Which one, which won (*and she begins to giggle*). This one.

OLIVER: She is ugly but not the same, I don't know her name she is ugly all the same, but she is not she, so I must not be scared when she says this you see.

MURIEL: If I say one two three and she is she she will look at me. (*She puts her head out and she calls out very loud*) One two three if you are she then look at me.

The old woman pays no attention but goes on picking up and throwing away sticks, always repeating.

APPARITION: One stick is one, this one, two sticks are two for which one, three sticks are three, suits me, four sticks are four, no more. Four sticks are four, three sticks are three, two sticks are two, one stick is one.

SUSIE: Oh Silly she scares me.

SILLY: Don't be silly but she scares me too.

SUSIE: Ouch.

SILLY: Ouch.

Both together: We wish we were brave but we are not, not, not, not.

Just then the old woman says:

APPARITION: One stick is one (*and she suddenly hits Oliver on the back*).

APPARITION: One stick is one whack on the back.

OLIVER: Oh oh, I am in two oh in two in two. It is only the string holds me together. Oh.

The old woman then hits Muriel on the back shouting:

APPARITION: Two sticks are two take that.

MURIEL (*dropping both bottles of milk which smash*): Oh I am getting thin it is most distressing, my milk, my milk, my ring oh I am getting so thin.

APPARITION (*behind Silly*): Three sticks are three (*and gives him a whack*).

SILLY: Oh I am not Silly I am only Willy and I do not want to be Willy I want to be Silly, oh.

Apparition goes behind Susie.

Four sticks are four and there are no more whack on your back.

SUSIE: Oh I am an egg, a white egg, not even a brown egg, a dirty white egg and it is addled and never now can I wed with dear Silly who is only Willy.

And they all throw themselves on the ground lamenting and the old woman dances away singing:

APPARITION: One stick is one two sticks are two three sticks are three four sticks are four, four sticks are four, three sticks are three two sticks are two one stick is one and now I am done.

OLIVER: I'll see to it that she never comes back.

MURIEL: Oh oh.

OLIVER (*grimly*): I'll see to it that she never comes back, the ugly, I am in two but she will never get through to us again.

MURIEL: I am so thin, my ring my ring, I am so thin.

SUSIE AND SILLY: Oh oh.

The curtain falls.

ACT III

Enter Oliver this time beside the string he has sticking plaster all down the front and the back of him holding him together and in his hand a large cardboard and wire and pincers.

Muriel coming in with a doll's carriage filled with butter sugar milk and bread. Susie is a large white egg and Silly is Willy. They come in slowly looking all around and sadly shaking their heads.

OLIVER: I may be a twin but she will never get in.

MURIEL: Oh dear I am getting so thin, I eat milk and bread and sugar and butter and they say of butter, one pound of butter makes two pounds of girl and oh dear butter, butter, I get thinner and thinner and my ring oh dear I am so thin.

SUSIE: Oh I wish I was a fish and not an egg and then I could swim and not do anything.

SILLY: I wish I wish I was not Willie, I wish I wish I wish I was Silly so I could marry Susie oh dear.

OLIVER (*darkly*): Well wait she cannot get in, see what I am doing.

He commences to stop up the entrance between the trees with wire and in the middle of it he puts a large sign NO TRESPASSING.

OLIVER: There what do I care if I am a twin, she never will get in never never.

MURIEL: Oh dear I am so thin, it is not interesting, oh dear I am so thin, oh dear where is my ring. I slip through my ring oh dear I am so thin.

SUSIE AND SILLY: Oh dear oh dear.

Just then the apparition appears disguised as a french poodle. She comes along barking and jumping.

OLIVER: Oh what a pretty dog. Dogs lick wounds and they heal perhaps he could lick me where I am in two and then I would be one, oh happy me not to be two but one. Which one. Oh happy day. Which one. One. One. One.

MURIEL: And perhaps he has a bone, bones make you fat oh it is that, I want to be fat, being thin is not interesting, being fat oh I want to be that.

SUSIE: Oh Willie sit on me quick it would be awful if he bit.

WILLY: If he bit he might make me Silly instead of Billy.

The poodle comes in barking and rushing around and they all say:

and what a pretty dog. I would like a pretty dog like that.

The dog comes up to Oliver barking and jumping.

APPARITION: Am I pretty am I witty and would you like to have a dog like that.

OLIVER: You bet I would, I'd give my hat, I'd give my bat to have a pretty dog like that.

APPARITION (*to Muriel*): Am I pretty am I witty and would you like to have a pretty dog like that.

MURIEL: Thin or fat I would oh I would like to have a pretty dog like that and I would make him a pretty hat of roses and daisies if I had a pretty dog like that.

APPARITION *to Susie and Silly* (*Willie is sitting on Susie*): Am I pretty am I witty and would you like a pretty dog like that.

SUSIE AND SILLY: We would that.

Apparition barking and dancing licks Oliver up and down saying:

I lick you front and back do you feel that.

OLIVER: You bet I do and it tickles too but it is funny now I know I am one and not two, thank you, thanks pretty doggie thanks for that.

Apparition kisses Muriel.

MURIEL: Oh happy day oh little by little I am getting fat, a pound to-day, not like yesterday, a pound every day oh I am getting fat. Oh thank you witty pretty doggie thank you for that.

Apparition jumps over Willie and Susie and they scream.

Oh we are Susie and we are Silly and thanks pretty dog for that.

Oliver goes over to the wire and takes down the cardboard NO TRESPASSING *and gives it to the dog who begs and takes it and dances with it tearing it up while the four cousins dance around the dog singing:*

The doggie is pretty the doggie is witty we all always want to have a dog like that.

[CURTAIN]